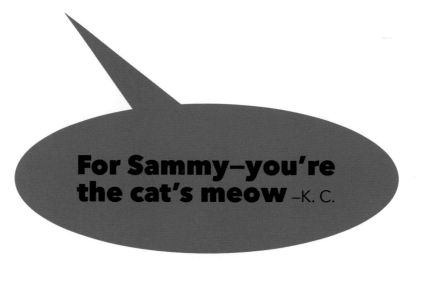

For Sammy—you're the cat's meow –K. C.

For Betts –B. J. S

Text copyright © 2021 by Kirsti Call
Illustrations copyright © 2021 by Brandon James Scott

All rights reserved. For information about permission to reproduce selections from this book, write to trade.permissions@hmhco.com or to Permissions, Houghton Mifflin Harcourt Publishing Company, 3 Park Avenue, 19th Floor, New York, New York 10016.

hmhbooks.com

The illustrations in this book were done in Photoshop with digital brushes.
The text was set in Avenir Next and Avenir Next Heavy.
Book design by Stephanie Hays

ISBN 978-0-358-42334-8

Manufactured in China
LEO 10 9 8 7 6 5 4 3 2 1
4500814861

COW SAYS

MEOW

Written by
KIRSTI CALL

Illustrated by
BRANDON JAMES SCOTT

HOUGHTON MIFFLIN HARCOURT
BOSTON   NEW YORK

Cow says . . .

Cat says . . .

NEIGH

The cat sounds hoarse!

Horse says . . .

I can't bear it.

Bear says . . .

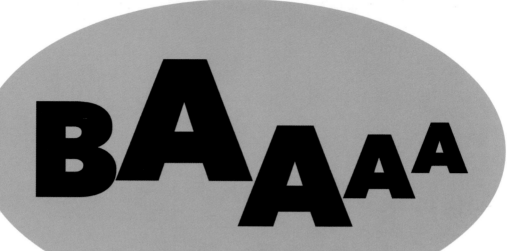

Sheep says . . .

WHOO
WHOO

Who's in charge of
this story anyway?

Owl says . . .

WOOF

You're barking up
the wrong tree!

Dog says . . .

Hen says . . .

Lion says . . .

Pig says . . .

Kid says . . .